Pout-Pout Fish
Easter Surprise

Written by **Wes Adams** Illustrated by **Isidre Monés**

Based on the *New York Times*–bestselling Pout-Pout Fish books
written by Deborah Diesen and illustrated by Dan Hanna

Farrar Straus Giroux
New York

Farrar Straus Giroux Books for Young Readers
An imprint of Macmillan Publishing Group, LLC
175 Fifth Avenue, New York, NY 10010

Color separations by Embassy Graphics
Printed in China by RR Donnelley Asia Printing Solutions Ltd., Dongguan City, Guandong Province
Designed by Aram Kim
First edition, 2018
10 9 8 7 6 5 4 3 2 1

mackids.com

Library of Congress Control Number: 2018936539
ISBN: 978-0-374-31051-6

Our books may be purchased in bulk for promotional, educational, or business use.
Please contact your local bookseller or the Macmillan Corporate and Premium Sales Department
at (800) 221-7945 ext. 5442 or by e-mail at MacmillanSpecialMarkets@macmillan.com.

Pout-Pout Fish

Mr. Fish was bubbling with excitement. The Easter-Egg Hunt was today!

But Mr. Fish was also worried. Every year, no matter how hard he hunted, he never came home with any eggs.

He found Mr. Eight and Mrs. Squid weaving baskets for everyone in the neighborhood.

"That looks like fun," said Mr. Fish. "Is there anything I can do to help?"

"Thanks for offering," said the octopus, finishing up several different baskets at once, "but we've got it covered."

"It's tricky business, Mr. Fish," said Mrs. Squid as her tentacles twisted and tied.

"Why don't you spread the word that we are ready to begin?" asked Mr. Eight.

Mr. Fish happily darted here and there, relaying the message to his friends.

Swimming to the school,
he found Miss Hewitt watching
over the little ones at recess. She sounded
the bell and the students lined up.

“Are you as excited as I am, Mr. Fish?” a little fry asked.

“I am *very* excited,” said Mr. Fish. He didn’t reveal that he was also *very* worried.

As everyone gathered, Mr. Fish resolved that he
wouldn't come home with an empty basket this year.

Soon the hunt was under way.
Mr. Fish found himself next to Miss Shimmer.
“How’s it going?” he asked his friend.

"No luck yet!" said Miss Shimmer.

Mr. Fish spotted a beautiful egg nestled in a grove of seagrass. Its decorations were dazzling.

"That one is perfect for you, Miss Shimmer!" exclaimed Mr. Fish.

"Why, thank you, Mr. Fish," said Miss Shimmer. "May I give you a smooch?"

"Yes!"

As the hunt continued, Mr. Fish swam this way and that. Near a shipwreck, he spied an egg that seemed just right—for his friend Starfish.

Underneath a coral reef, he uncovered a pearly white beauty for Ms. Clam.

With Mr. Lantern, Mr. Fish explored a dark crevasse and found an egg with a glow all its own.

"This one is very you," Mr. Fish said to his luminescent friend.

More and
more eggs were
discovered, and
the treasure hunt was
winding down. And then,
to his surprise, Mr. Fish
discovered an egg of his
very own . . .

. . . but then he saw the friendly little fry,
who hadn't found any eggs yet.

“I’ve been saving this one for you,” said Mr. Fish, turning her pout into a smile.

“That was very kind of you,” Miss Hewitt said, and everyone around agreed.

Mr. Fish had a wonderful, warm feeling inside that chased away his worry.

“It’s really nothing,”
he said with a smile
of his own.

But Pout-Pout Fish's friends and neighbors didn't think it was nothing. They thought it was something. Something very wonderful indeed.

Before Mr. Fish could swim away home with an empty basket once again, they surprised him with a special treat they'd gathered just for him.

"You always help us find the perfect eggs," said Mr. Eight. "And we wanted to make sure you found the perfect treasure for yourself."

“I don’t know what to say,” said Mr. Fish.

“There’s only one thing to say,” said the little fry.

"HAPPY EASTER, POUT-POUT FISH!"

The author would like to thank everyone who has helped with this book, and with special thanks to Ernie and Mavis Davis; Nancy Mary Goodall; M.D. How & Son, Chesham, Bucks; Caroline Lushington; Sue Miller; Whitbread & Company PLC (Whitbread Hop Farm, Paddock Wood, Kent).

SIMON & SCHUSTER BOOKS FOR YOUNG READERS
Simon & Schuster Building, Rockefeller Center, 1230 Avenue of the Americas, New York, New York 10020. First U.S. edition 1989.
Originated by J. M. Dent & Sons Ltd.
First published in Great Britain in 1988.

SIMON & SCHUSTER BOOKS FOR YOUNG READERS is a trademark of Simon & Schuster.
Manufactured in the United States of America
10 9 8 7 6 5 4 3 2 1
10 9 8 7 6 5 4 3 2 1 (pbk)
Library of Congress Cataloging-in-Publication Data
Miller, Jane, 1925-. Farm noises. Summary: Presents the distinctive sounds made by two dozen animals, birds, and machines that may be heard on farms. 1. Farm sounds—Juvenile literature. [1. Animal noises. 2. Bird song. 3. Farm sounds] I. Title.
5519.M549 1986- 363'01 88-18540
ISBN: 0-671-67450-1 ISBN: 0-671-75976-0 (pbk)

For Edward

FARM NOISES

JANE MILLER

Simon & Schuster Books for Young Readers
Published by Simon & Schuster
New York • London • Toronto • Sydney • Tokyo • Singapore

Roosters crow:
cock-a-doodle-doo

Hens cluck.
Chicks cheep

Donkeys bray:
ee-aw

Horses neigh and snort

Sheep and lambs baa

Crows call:
kaaah kaaah kaaah

Bees buzz-z-z-z
z-z-z

Mice squeak:
ee-ee-ee

Pigs grunt:
oink oink oink

Piglets squeal

Dogs bark and growl:
wuff-wuff, grrr-grrr
Puppies yap

Cats and kittens
meow and purr

Birds sing
and chirp

Frogs croak:
rib-it rib-it rib-it

Ducks and ducklings
go quack-quack

Streams gurgle

Bulls bellow

Cows moo

Combine harvesters roar

Tractors go
brum-brum

Geese honk.
Goslings cheep

Some owls hoot: tu-wit tu-whoo.
But barn owls shriek

Goats bleat:
maa-maa

And turkeys go
gobble-gobble